Salty and Button

Written by Angela McAllister

illustrated by Tiphanie Beeke

MACMILLAN CHILDREN'S BOOKS

Salty and Button loved to play pirates.
Salty searched for adventures with his
telescope and made up games about shipwrecks
and sharks. He was always the hero.

Button used his sewing bag to make
them costumes and flags. He sang songs
about treasure islands.

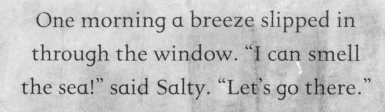

One morning a breeze slipped in
through the window. "I can smell
the sea!" said Salty. "Let's go there."

Button wasn't sure.
"The sea is full of sharks and
shipwrecks," he said.

"But it smells exciting!" said Salty.
"It smells like real adventure!"

Button didn't want a real adventure, but he
didn't want to be left alone. So he packed
his sewing bag and his warm blanket and
took Salty's hand.

They followed the breeze until they came to the beach.
There before them was the sparkling sea.

"How exciting," gasped Salty.
But Button covered up his ears.
"It's too loud," he said. "It's too rough."

Salty found a shell boat and a driftwood paddle.
"All aboard for a pirate adventure," he cried.

The sea looks big and wild, thought Button,
but he didn't want to be left alone. So he held
Salty's hand tight and stepped in.

Salty paddled a little way and peered through
his telescope. "Shark fins!" he cried.
"Let's take a closer look."

"Oh dear," gasped Button.
"I don't want to meet a shark."

"Be brave, shipmate," said Salty.
"This is a real adventure."

But when they got close, they saw
that the fins were only seagulls.

They paddled a little further, then Salty
looked through his telescope again.
"A pirate ship!" he cried. "Let's have a battle."

"Oh dear," said Button.
"I don't want to meet a pirate."

"Don't worry," said Salty. "I'll be the hero."

But when they got close they found that the
pirate ship was just a craggy rock.

On and on they rowed, far away from
the beach and far away from home.

Dark clouds began to roll across the sky.
Then thunder rumbled and rain began to fall.
"This adventure's too scary," said Button.
"I want to go home."

All of a sudden an enormous wave tipped the boat
and Salty tumbled into the water.

"Help!" he spluttered.

The sea swirled around Salty and tugged him away.

"Come back!" cried Button.

But Salty floated out of sight and Button was left all alone.

Then Button remembered the telescope . . .

He searched the wide ocean until there, far in the
distance, he spotted Salty bobbing on the waves.

"I've got to be a brave shipmate,"
Button told himself. "I have to rescue Salty."

So he began to paddle with all his might.
"I'll save you, Salty," he cried.

It was a long way and soon his arms began to ache.
But at last Button was close enough!
He reached out to Salty . . . stretching . . .
and stretching . . . until . . .

Salty grabbed Button's hand and
scrambled back into the boat.

Poor, wet Salty didn't feel like a hero any more.
"This adventure's too scary," he said.
"I want to go home."

But which way was home?
Where was the beach?

"Oh, Button," he cried. "We're lost!"

"Be brave, shipmate," said Button.
"I have an idea."

Button took out his sewing things
and set to work.

Before long he had made a beautiful blanket sail
and together they fixed it to the paddle.

"Do you remember the sea breeze that blew all
the way into our house?" asked Button.
"Maybe it can take us home . . ."

At once the wind filled Button's sail
and the boat set off across the waves.

"Now we're a pirate galleon," laughed Salty.

Soon the storm rolled away and the sun came out.

"Land ahoy!" cried Button.

At last they stepped back onto the beach.
"Thank you for saving me, Button," said Salty.
"You are a true hero."

Button squeezed Salty's hand.
"I'm glad we had a real adventure," he said.
"But I like our pirate games best."

"So do I," Salty agreed.

And so the two weary friends said
goodbye to the sea . . .

and sang pirate songs all the way home.